HAMSTE

Also in the Animal Ark Pets Series

LAURA WRIGHT

LUCY DANIELS
Hamster
Holiday

Illustrated by Paul Howard

Hodder
Children's
Books

a division of Hodder Headline Limited

Special thanks to Narinder Dhami

Animal Ark is a trademark of Working Partners Limited
Text copyright © 2001 Working Partners Limited,
Created by Working Partners Limited, London W6 OQT
Original series created by Ben M. Baglio
Illustrations copyright © 2001 Paul Howard
Cover illustration by Chris Chapman

First published in Great Britain in 2001
by Hodder Children's Books

A Catalogue record for this book is available from the British Library

ISBN 0 340 85269 0

Typeset by Avon Dataset Ltd, Bidford-on-Avon, Warks

Printed and bound in Great Britain by
The Guernsey Press Co. Ltd, Channel Isles

Hodder Children's Books
a division of Hodder Headline Limited
338 Euston Road
London NW1 3BH

Contents

Contents

1

A Special Announcement

"I'm so excited, James!" Mandy Hope whispered in her best friend's ear. She was trying hard to sit still, but it was very difficult.

"Me too," James whispered back. "And I don't know if I can wait until the Christmas Fair to find out your gran's secret!"

Mandy nodded. She and James Hunter were sitting at the front of the school hall, while the rest of Welford Primary School filed in quietly. Mandy and James had a very special announcement to make at the end of carol practice, which was why they were sitting together at the front.

Just then, Oliver Morgan from Class Six walked over and sat down next to them. Oliver must have an announcement to make too, Mandy thought. She wondered what it could be. She and James didn't know Oliver very well. The Morgans had only moved to Welford in September, and they didn't have any pets, as far as Mandy knew. At any rate, she'd never seen them at Animal Ark.

Mandy's parents were both vets, and they worked from a surgery which was built on to the back of their house in Welford. Mandy knew almost all the pets in Welford.

James nudged her. "Here's Mrs Garvie," he said in a low voice.

Everyone stood up as the headmistress walked into the hall and stepped on to the platform. "Good morning, everyone," she said with a smile. "We'll start with 'Once in Royal David's City'."

As everyone began to sing, Mandy felt even more excited. It was nearly the end of the winter term, and it wasn't long to Christmas. Yesterday, Mandy and James had helped Mrs Hope decorate two Christmas trees, one for the Hopes' living-room and a smaller one for the surgery waiting-room. Mandy grinned as she remembered how they'd decorated the surgery with packets of cat treats and dog biscuits tied up with ribbon.

After they'd sung two carols, Mrs Garvie read a story about a donkey at Christmas. Mandy was so interested in the story she almost forgot that she and James had an important announcement to make until Mrs Garvie looked over at them.

"Now, we have some very special news for you this morning," the headmistress said briskly. "First, Mandy Hope and James Hunter would like to talk to you." Mrs Garvie smiled at Mandy and James as they climbed on to the platform.

Mandy cleared her throat, feeling herself turn pink as she looked out over the sea of faces. "It's about the Women's Institute Christmas Fair on the twenty-third of December," she began, speaking slowly so that she didn't get the words muddled up. "James and I will be helping my gran to run a cake stall, and we want loads of people to come along because the fair is in aid of the RSPCA this year."

"And Mandy's gran's cakes are great!" James put in helpfully. Then he blushed, as there was a ripple of laughter round the hall.

"We're not just going to be selling cakes, either," Mandy went on. "We've got a special animal section where we'll be selling home-made pet treats and wild bird food and all sorts of other stuff."

"I bet that was Mandy's idea!" laughed Richard Tanner, who was in Mandy's class. Everyone knew Mandy was mad about animals.

Mandy couldn't help smiling. It *had* been her idea, as a matter of fact. Quickly she nudged James. "Tell them about Gran's surprise," she whispered.

"And best of all, we'll have two very special guests on our stall," James announced importantly, pushing his glasses further up his nose. "We can't tell you who they are though – it's such a secret that we don't even know ourselves! You'll have to come along to the Village Hall and find out!"

"All that Gran will say is that our special guests will be part of a competition to win a really *huge* Christmas cake that she's made," Mandy added.

Everyone in the hall started whispering excitedly to each other, until Mrs Garvie held up her hand for silence. "Thank you, Mandy and James," she said.

It looked as if their announcement about the two special guests had really caused a stir, Mandy thought happily, as she and James sat down again. Everyone seemed so excited, she wouldn't be surprised if the whole of Welford Primary turned up at the Christmas Fair! She just wished her gran would let *her* in on the secret too.

"And now we have another announcement

from Oliver Morgan," Mrs Garvie went on.

Oliver stood up and climbed on to the platform. Mandy could see that he looked a bit nervous. "It's about my hamster camp," he began, shuffling from one foot to the other and shaking his fair hair out of his eyes.

Mandy glanced at James. A hamster camp? That sounded interesting.

"I'm planning to run it over the Christmas holidays," Oliver went on. "It's for hamster owners who are going away and can't take their pets with them. They can leave their hamsters with me, and I'll look after them."

James raised his eyebrows at Mandy. "That's a good idea," he whispered.

It seemed like the rest of the school thought so too, Mandy noticed. There was almost as much chattering going on as when she and James had made *their* announcement.

"Or if anyone's got lots of noisy relatives staying over Christmas, they might want to send their hamster to me for some peace and quiet!" Oliver added, and everyone laughed.

"So you're a hamster expert, are you, Oliver?" Mrs Garvie said, looking amused.

"Well, I've looked after hamsters before, lots of times," Oliver replied.

"Then I'm sure they'll be in good hands," Mrs Garvie said. "And if anyone thinks their hamster deserves a holiday over Christmas, they can speak to Oliver about it. Now, it's almost playtime, so can you go outside quietly, please. Class Six, you can go first."

Mandy leaned closer to James as they waited their turn to file out. "Do you think Oliver might need some help with his hamster camp?" she whispered. "If he's looking after a lot of hamsters at once, some of them might get a bit poorly," she pointed out. "Maybe I should tell him about Animal Ark."

"Good idea," James said. "Why don't we go and say hello to him at playtime?"

"OK," Mandy agreed. She thought Oliver's idea of a hamster camp was brilliant. And if Animal Ark could help to keep all his hamster guests safe and healthy, then that was even better . . .

2
Exciting Plans

"Look, James." Mandy nudged her friend as they went out into the playground. "I think Oliver's hamster camp is going to be a big success."

James grinned. Oliver was standing in the middle of the playground with a small crowd of children clustered around him. Oliver was writing down their names in a notebook.

"That's Karen Smythe, from my class," said James, pointing out a tall girl standing next to Oliver. "Hasn't she got a hamster called Pinky?"

Mandy nodded. "And there's Daniel Burton, from Class Six. He's got two dwarf Russian hamsters, Milly and Mungo."

"I hope Oliver isn't going to be overrun with hamsters," James laughed. "It looks like every hamster in Welford will be going to the hamster camp over Christmas."

"So it's even more important for us to tell Oliver about Animal Ark," Mandy said. "Look, Oliver's on his own now. Let's go over and say hello."

Oliver was sitting on the wall at the edge of the playground, flipping through his notebook. He looked up with a smile as Mandy and James walked up to him. "Hello, are you interested in the hamster camp too?" he asked.

"Not exactly!" Mandy smiled back. "I haven't got a hamster."

"And neither have I," James added. "Just a cat called Benji and a Labrador puppy called Blackie."

Oliver's face lit up. "I love dogs," he said eagerly. "I'm saving up to buy a Golden Retriever puppy, that's why I'm running the hamster camp. But I love hamsters too. My mum says I'm animal mad."

"That's funny," Mandy laughed. "That's what mine says about me."

"You're Mandy Hope, aren't you?" Oliver said. "From Animal Ark?"

Mandy nodded. "And this is my best friend, James," she explained. "We thought you might need some help with the hamsters, so we decided to tell you about my mum and dad's surgery. But it looks like you've heard about us already!"

"Everybody in Welford knows about Animal Ark." Oliver grinned. "But thanks for telling me. If any of the hamsters get ill, I'll know where to come."

"So how do you know so much about hamsters, Oliver?" James asked. He sat down next to him on the wall. "Have you got one of your own?"

"No, but when we lived in our old house, I

used to look after our neighbours' hamsters all the time." Oliver replied. "They had ten of them."

"*Ten!*" Mandy and James repeated, their eyes wide.

"Yes, I looked after them while my neighbours were on holiday." Oliver took a bag of crisps from his pocket, opened it, and offered some to Mandy and James. "One time, two of the hamsters had babies, and when their owners came home, I gave them back seventeen hamsters instead of ten!"

Mandy and James laughed. "I love hamster babies," Mandy said. "I think they look like wrinkled baked beans!"

"Have you got many bookings for the hamster camp yet?" James asked.

Oliver shook his head. "I haven't got any definite bookings yet," he replied. "There are a lot of people who're interested, and I've written their names down. But they've got to ask their parents first."

"Where are you going to be keeping the hamsters?" Mandy asked curiously. Hamsters usually had to be kept in separate cages, so Oliver would need plenty of space if he had lots of hamster guests.

"My mum and dad have said I can keep them in the loft," Oliver explained. "It's just been decorated and the builders have put radiators in, so it's warm and cosy."

"Wow!" James's mouth fell open. "Your parents must love animals too if they're letting you keep the hamsters in a room that's just been decorated!"

"Well, it's the only place in the house that's

been finished," Oliver replied. "It's being done up so everything's in a bit of a mess at the moment. That's why I can't have a dog yet. Mum says I've got to wait until the house is sorted."

"So the hamsters will be getting the best room in the house!" James joked.

Oliver nodded. "We haven't got any carpets down yet, and the floorboards are up in some of the rooms," he went on. "And there are pots of paint and decorating stuff lying around. I want to keep the hamsters away from all that."

"It sounds like the loft's probably the safest place then," Mandy agreed. She glanced at James. It looked as if Oliver was taking his hamster camp responsibilities very seriously indeed.

"Well, good luck, Oliver," said Mandy as the bell rang for the end of playtime. She jumped off the wall and brushed crisp crumbs off her skirt. "I hope you get lots of guests at your hamster camp."

"I'm sure you will," James added. "Lots of people at Welford Primary have got hamsters."

"Oh, the hamster camp isn't just for people at school," Oliver said with a grin. "It's for everyone in Welford and Walton, too. My mum's put up a notice about it in the window of the estate agents where she works, and I've put another notice in the pet shop in Walton."

"So you could have *hundreds* of hamsters coming to stay," Mandy teased.

"That'd be brilliant," Oliver said happily, "although I'm not sure Mum and Dad would be too pleased!" He glanced across at Mandy and James as they walked into school. "I'm going to spend this weekend getting the loft ready for the hamster camp," he went on hesitantly. "Would you two like to give me a hand?"

Mandy and James both looked thrilled. "We'd love to," Mandy said, her eyes shining.

"Great!" Oliver said. "Are you sure you won't be too busy with this Christmas Fair?"

Mandy shook her head. "The holidays start next week, so we'll have plenty of time for the fair."

"And what about the two special guests?"

Oliver asked curiously. "Will they keep you busy?"

Mandy and James looked at each other and shrugged. "To tell you the truth, we're not sure," Mandy said. "Gran refuses to tell us anything about it! She's doing really well at keeping them a secret."

Oliver grinned. "I suppose we'll *all* just have to wait and see," he said. "I'll see you on Saturday morning then."

"We'll be there!" Mandy said with a smile.

"There's a lot going on, isn't there?" James said happily, as he and Mandy walked home through Welford later that afternoon. It was already getting dark and the air was cold and frosty. "Helping Oliver prepare for the hamster camp this weekend, then all the Christmas parties at school next week, and then the Christmas Fair."

"And we haven't even got to Christmas yet!" Mandy laughed. "Come on, we said we'd pop in and help Gran on the way home." She tucked the soft blue scarf her Gran had knitted firmly into her coat. "It's getting cold, isn't it, James?"

"Yes, I bet the hamsters will be glad that the Morgans' loft is nice and warm," James remarked.

"I hope Oliver's hamster camp is a big success," Mandy said, as they turned in the direction of Lilac Cottage. "He's so excited about it, it would be a shame if he didn't get any guests."

"Maybe Oliver will have had his first booking by the time we go over there tomorrow morning," James suggested, opening the gate to Lilac Cottage.

"I hope so," Mandy replied.

They walked up the path and rang the bell. A moment later, Mandy's grandad opened the door. "Ah, there you are," he said, with a broad smile. "Come on in, out of the cold."

Mandy and James hurried inside the cosy cottage and started peeling off the layers of coats, hats, scarves and gloves they both wore.

"Yum!" James whispered, sniffing the air. "Your gran's been baking."

"Yes, Dorothy's already started making cakes for the Christmas Fair," said Grandad Hope, overhearing. He led them into the kitchen, where a delicious-looking lemon sponge and a huge pile of currant buns were on the table. Grandad's eyes twinkled, as he saw the hungry look on James's face. "I'm sure she wouldn't notice if two buns went missing!" He handed one bun to James and one to Mandy.

"Thanks, Mr Hope," James said gratefully, taking a big bite.

"Isn't it too early to start baking cakes yet?" Mandy asked. "The fair isn't for another week."

"Well, your gran's going to pop these into the freezer," Grandad replied. "It means we'll have less to do next week."

"Good idea," James said, finishing off his bun. Mandy tucked into hers, too. As usual, her gran's baking was delicious. "Where *is* Gran anyway?" she asked, looking round the kitchen.

"She's gone to do some shopping," Grandad replied. "So in the meantime I thought we'd get on with a bit of baking of our own for the fair." He held up a leaflet called *Homemade Bird Treats*.

"Oh, brilliant!" Mandy exclaimed. "Have we got everything we need, Grandad?"

Grandad nodded. "It's all here," he said, waving his hand towards one of the kitchen worktops. It was covered with a tempting array of ingredients, including oats, bits of chopped apple, peanut butter, suet and raisins, as well as a big packet of wild bird seed. There was also a muffin tin lined with greaseproof paper, and two large china bowls.

"We'll mix up the recipes in that bowl, and then put the mixture into the muffin tin," Grandad explained.

"And then we cook it?" James asked, looking puzzled.

"No, we just pop the tin into the fridge until the bird cakes have hardened," Grandad replied. "And we can use these too." He showed Mandy and James some empty milk cartons.

"I know what those are for!" Mandy said,

21

her face lighting up. "We pour the mixture into the carton, and then when it's hardened we can cut the sides out."

Her grandad nodded. "Then it can be hung up in the garden so the birds can get at the mixture easily." He handed Mandy and James two big aprons. "Put these on and let's get to work."

James fetched the mixing bowls and two wooden spoons, while Mandy helped Grandad measure out the ingredients.

"Mmm, I wouldn't mind a taste of this," James remarked as he tipped some peanut butter into his bowl and mixed it with some oats and apple.

Mandy laughed. "Just remember to leave some for the poor old birds, James!"

By the time Mandy's gran arrived with her shopping, Mandy and James had already filled the muffin tin, as well as four milk cartons, and were putting them in the fridge to chill.

"Look what we've made, Gran," Mandy said proudly, showing her the bird cakes.

"And Mr Hope says we can freeze them so

that they'll stay nice and fresh for the fair,"
James added. "Just like *your* cakes."

"Well done." Mandy's gran beamed at them
as she took off her coat. "That's a good start."

Mandy grinned. "Are you sure you won't
tell us who the mystery guests are yet, Gran?"
she asked hopefully.

"Good try Mandy!" Gran laughed. "But I'm
afraid you'll just have to wait until the Fair
along with everybody else." Then she frowned.

"There's so much to do, I just hope we manage to finish everything—'

"Don't start worrying now, Dorothy," Grandad interrupted her, winking at Mandy. "We've got plenty of time before the fair. Now, haven't you got something you wanted to show Mandy and James?"

Gran's eyes began to twinkle. "I certainly have," she said, going over to one of the cupboards. "What do you think of *these*?" She took some biscuit-cutters out of the cupboard, and laid them on the table.

Puzzled, Mandy took a closer look, and then began to laugh. The biscuit-cutters were all shaped like animals. There was a dog, a cat, a rabbit, a pig and a sheep. "Oh, Gran," Mandy gasped. "They're brilliant! Can James and I make some animal-shaped biscuits?"

Her gran nodded. "Of course you can."

James nudged Mandy. "Pity there's not a *hamster*, though!" he whispered.

Mandy burst out laughing, while Gran and Grandad looked puzzled. Quickly James explained about Oliver Morgan's hamster camp. ". . . And now Oliver's waiting to see how many hamsters come to stay," James finished.

"Oh!" Mandy said suddenly. "I've just had an idea, Gran. What about Frisky? Do you think Mary might be going away again this year?"

Frisky the hamster belonged to Mary, a friend of Mandy's grandparents. Earlier this year, Mary had asked them to look after Frisky for her while she was away. Mandy had moved into Lilac Cottage to help. She'd become very fond of the lively little Russian hamster.

"Mary might be going away," Gran said thoughtfully. "She hasn't asked us to look after Frisky, but then she knows how busy we are with the Christmas Fair. I'll ask her. She might be very interested in Oliver's hamster camp."

James grinned at Mandy. "You might just have found Oliver his first guest!"

"Let's hope so," Mandy replied eagerly.

3

Hamsters Galore!

"A hamster camp?" Adam Hope raised his eyebrows at Mandy, who was finishing off her cornflakes. It was Saturday morning, and the Hopes were having breakfast. "Are the hamsters going to be living in tents?"

"Oh, *Dad!*" Mandy groaned, trying not to giggle. "Oliver's going to keep the hamster cages in the loft. There's loads of space, and it's nice and warm."

"I think it's a wonderful idea," Emily Hope joined in. She poured herself another cup of tea. "As long as Oliver knows how to look after hamsters properly, there shouldn't be any problem."

"Oh, he does," Mandy said quickly. She explained how Oliver had regularly looked after his neighbours' hamsters. "Gran thinks Mary might be interested."

"Well, even Frisky on his own would keep Oliver busy!" Mr Hope joked as he folded up his newspaper. "Are you ready, Mandy?" Mr Hope was driving Mandy over to the Morgans' house, and they were picking up James on the way.

"Yes, I am." Mandy pushed her cereal bowl away. "And Dad, can we stop off at Lilac Cottage too? I want to see if Gran's spoken to Mary yet."

Mr Hope nodded and Mandy rushed off to get her coat. As they were climbing into the Land Rover, Mandy's mum hurried out, clutching a bunch of leaflets from the surgery.

"Oliver might find these useful," she said with a smile, 'even if he *is* a hamster expert!"

Mandy wound the window down and took the leaflets, which were all about caring for hamsters. "Thanks, Mum." She waved as her dad reversed the Land Rover, and they set off through Welford.

James was looking out of the window of his living-room as they turned into his drive. He came running out of the front door followed by Blackie, who just managed to squeeze through the door before James closed it. "Bad boy, Blackie!" James shouted, as the puppy spotted Mandy and dashed towards the Land Rover, his tail wagging madly. "Come here this minute!"

Mandy couldn't help laughing as James scooped up his naughty pup and carried him back to the house.

"Sorry about that, Mr Hope," James gasped, as he climbed into the Land-rover beside Mandy. "Blackie hates it if I go anywhere without him."

"Yes, I can see that, James!" Mandy's dad grinned.

"We're going to call in at Lilac Cottage before we go to the Morgans' house," Mandy told James. "Gran might have spoken to Mary about the hamster camp."

"And then we might be able to tell Oliver that Frisky's going to be one of his guests." James beamed. "Brilliant!"

"Don't get too excited," Mr Hope warned them, as he drew up outside Lilac Cottage. "Mary might not be going away this year."

Mandy's gran answered the door, and her face lit up when she saw them. "Well, look who's here!" she exclaimed. "The very people I wanted to see. Mary's popped round for a cup of tea, and I've just been telling her all about the hamster camp."

"Is she interested, Gran?" Mandy asked eagerly.

"Come in and ask her yourself," Gran replied, leading them through to the kitchen.

Mary, a small, grey-haired woman with bright blue eyes, was sitting at the table with

30

Grandad, sipping her tea. She smiled at Mandy and James. "Hello, you two," she said. "Dorothy's been telling me all about this hamster camp of yours."

"Well, it's not really *ours*," James said. "We're just helping Oliver Morgan to get it ready."

"Are you going away this year, Mary?" Mandy asked. She couldn't wait to find out if Oliver was about to get his first booking.

Mary nodded. "I'm going to see some friends in Derbyshire."

"So would you like Frisky to go to the hamster camp?" Mandy suggested hopefully.

Mary frowned. "Well, I think it's a lovely idea," she said slowly, 'but I have to make sure that Frisky's looked after properly. If Oliver's caring for a lot of hamsters, they may not all get the attention they need."

"Oliver's used to looking after lots of hamsters at a time," Mandy explained quickly.

"And Animal Ark will be on hand in case there are any problems," Adam Hope added. "But I'm sure there won't be. From what Mandy tells us, Oliver sounds like a very responsible lad."

"Well, it *would* solve the problem of who'll look after Frisky while I'm away," Mary admitted. "I didn't want to ask your grandparents again, Mandy, because I know they're so busy with the fair. Do you know how much Oliver is charging for the hamster camp?"

Mandy looked uncertain. "I don't know, actually," she confessed. Then she brightened up. "But I'm sure it won't be very much, and it's for a very good cause – Oliver is saving up to buy a puppy!"

Mary laughed. "Well, in that case . . ." she began.

"So can I tell Oliver that Frisky will be coming to his camp?" Mandy burst out. She held her breath.

"Yes, I think you can," said Mary with a smile.

Mandy and James cheered loudly.

"I can't *wait*!" Mandy said happily, her eyes shining.

"That's great!" Oliver exclaimed when Mandy and James gave him the good news. "That's another one!"

"*Another* one?" Mandy echoed, her eyes wide.

Oliver nodded. "Daniel Burton rang last night and asked me if I would look after Milly and Mungo. *And* I had a call this morning from a lady in Walton. She wants me to look after Billy, her little boy's hamster."

"That's great," James said, stamping his feet

up and down on the doorstep in an effort to get warm. It was a bitterly cold and frosty morning.

"Sorry, you'd better come in before you freeze." Oliver opened the door wider. "I was so excited about Frisky, I forgot my manners!"

Mandy and James stepped gratefully inside the large hall. There were paint pots, brushes and dustsheets everywhere, and the walls had been stripped of paper. The floorboards were bare too.

"Dad, this is Mandy and James," Oliver said, as a tall, fair-haired man wearing silver-rimmed glasses came out of the living-room. He was holding the hand of a pretty little girl of about four, who had a mass of golden curls and big blue eyes.

"Hi, Mandy and James." Mr Morgan smiled at them. "I've heard a lot about you. And this is Tammy, Oliver's sister. Say hello, Tammy."

Tammy looked shy and tried to hide behind her father's legs.

"Mum's at work," Oliver explained. "She'll

be back at lunchtime so you'll meet her then."
He led them over to the stairs. "Come on,
let's go up to the loft."

Just then the phone rang.

"Dad, can I answer it?" Oliver asked eagerly.
"It might be someone ringing about the
hamster camp." Mr Morgan nodded, and
Oliver dashed over to the phone, which was
on a narrow table in the hallway.

Mandy and James watched eagerly as he
picked up the receiver.

"Hello?" Oliver said. "Oh, hello, Karen."

"I bet it's Karen Smythe," James whispered
to Mandy. "I bet she wants Pinky to join the
hamster camp!"

After talking to Karen for a few minutes,
Oliver put the phone down and gave Mandy
and James a thumbs-up sign. "I've got another
hamster!" he announced. But that was all he
had time to say before the phone rang again.
This time it was from a couple in Walton who
wanted Oliver to look after their hamster,
Herbert, while they were away.

"Your hamster camp is going to be full up at

this rate," Mandy laughed when Oliver put the phone down.

Oliver grinned. "There's quite a lot of room in the loft, but I don't think I could look after more than ten or eleven hamsters properly."

"How many have you got so far?" James asked, counting them up on his fingers. "Milly, Mungo, Frisky, Billy, Pinky and Herbert. That's six."

"Maybe this is going to be another one," Mr Morgan joked, as the doorbell rang. Then he glanced into the living-room and his smile faded. "Tammy, I've told you a hundred times not to touch the wet paint!" he said sternly. "Olly, will you get that?"

Oliver hurried over to the door and opened it.

A little girl about the same age as Tammy was standing there, holding her mum's hand. It was Mrs Milton and her daughter, Emma. Mandy recognised them because they'd been to Animal Ark several times with their hamster, Barney.

"Oh, are you Oliver Morgan?" Mrs Milton

asked. "We've come about the hamster camp. We want to book a place for our hamster, Barney."

Mandy and James grinned at each other as Oliver and Mrs Milton discussed the arrangements. The hamster camp was already a runaway success! It was going to mean a lot of hard work, though, Mandy thought.

"Phew!" Oliver shut the door after Emma and her mum had gone. He looked a bit dazed. "I never thought my hamster camp would be *this* popular."

"Maybe we'd better start getting the loft ready," Mandy suggested.

Oliver nodded. "Let's go upstairs," he said, leading them up the wide, uncarpeted staircase.

The house was on two floors and the loft was right at the top, reached by a spiral metal staircase.

"Wow!" James said admiringly. "This is brilliant!"

The loft was spacious and warm, and decorated in a soft yellow colour. The only furniture was a desk, a chair and a bookcase, but there were wide shelves all around the room on two levels, one at waist height and one a bit higher. There were three skylights in the roof to let light in, as well as one large window which overlooked Welford and the moors beyond. In one corner there was a pile of cardboard boxes, all of different sizes.

"Do you think it's OK for the hamsters?" Oliver asked anxiously.

"It's perfect!" Mandy said. "It's big, but it's really warm too."

"Where are you going to put the hamsters' cages?" James asked.

"On the shelves," Oliver replied. He pointed to a pile of dusters and some disinfectant spray on the desk. "I need to clean them first."

"Good idea," Mandy agreed. "And what are all those cardboard boxes for?"

"I thought we could cut them up and make a few hamster runs," Oliver explained. "Then I can let the hamsters out of their cages so that they can get some exercise." He looked serious for a moment. "One at a time, of course," he added. "I know hamsters fight if you put them together."

"We could make a couple of obstacle courses too," Mandy suggested. "Hamsters like that sort of thing."

"Come on, then." James grabbed a duster. "Let's get started."

They cleaned all the shelves carefully, then sat down to make the hamster runs. James and Oliver cut the ends out of the boxes while Mandy taped them together to make two long runs. While they were working, Tammy put her head shyly round the door and looked into the room.

"Hi, Tammy," Mandy said kindly. "Do you want to come and help us?"

Tammy nodded and toddled into the room, treading on some of the boxes Mandy had already taped together.

"Oh, *Tammy*!" Oliver sighed, rushing to rescue the hamster runs. "Sorry," he said to Mandy. "She can be a bit of a handful."

There was the sound of footsteps on the stairs, and the next moment a fair-haired woman with curls exactly like Tammy's came into the room.

"Oh, hi, Mum." Oliver looked surprised. "I didn't know it was lunchtime already."

"I got home about five minutes ago." Mrs Morgan smiled. "And this must be Mandy and James. Hello."

"Hello," Mandy and James said together.

"I see the preparations for the hamster camp are going well." Mrs Morgan hurried across the loft to grab Tammy, who'd climbed up on to the chair and was now standing on the desk. "Oliver, there's just been another phone call.

The McDonald family from Walton want you to look after their hamsters."

"Their *hamsters*?" Oliver asked. "How many?"

His mum raised her eyebrows at him. "Five babies," she said.

Oliver's eyes opened wide. "Five babies!" he gasped, glancing at Mandy and James. Mandy could understand why he looked a bit worried. That meant Oliver would be looking after *twelve* hamsters in total!

"The McDonalds are going to visit relatives in Scotland over Christmas," Mrs Morgan went on. "They're taking the hamster parents with them, but they think the babies are too young for such a long journey."

"How old are the hamsters, Mrs Morgan?" Mandy asked.

"About five weeks old, according to Mr McDonald," Oliver's mum replied.

"Well, that's not so bad." Mandy turned to Oliver. "They're still young enough to share the same cage."

"That's true," Oliver agreed. "Hamsters need

to be separated at about six weeks. Anyway, it looks like my hamster camp's full up! I just hope I can cope with all the feeding and cleaning-out."

"James and I will help you," Mandy offered.

Oliver beamed at her. "Would you? That'd be great. And I'll help you with the Christmas Fair, if you like."

"It's a deal," Mandy agreed with a smile.

4

The Guests Arrive

"Merry Christmas, Mrs Todd!" Mandy waved at her teacher and hurried out of the classroom. It was the last day of Christmas term at Welford Primary. The Christmas concerts and parties were over, and now everyone was looking forward to the holidays. Although, Mandy reminded herself, there was still *lots* to do before Christmas Day. Oliver's hamster camp was opening for business the following day, and Mandy and James were going over to help Oliver settle the hamsters in. Then there was the Christmas Fair in four days' time.

"Come on, Mandy!" James was waiting impatiently for her in the playground. "We said we'd go straight to Lilac Cottage. Your gran and grandad will be wondering where we are."

"Sorry," Mandy panted. "I was helping Mrs Todd clear up the classroom."

"It doesn't feel much like Christmas, does it?" James remarked, as they hurried through Welford. The weather had suddenly turned milder, and a pale sun was shining in the light-blue sky.

"Wait till you see all your presents." Mandy grinned at him. "Then it'll feel *just* like Christmas!"

"I bought some dog treats for Blackie and hung them on our tree," James told her, opening the gate to Lilac Cottage. "When I went back five minutes later, he'd managed to pull them off and eat the lot."

Mandy laughed. "Maybe Blackie couldn't wait for Father Christmas."

The kitchen inside Lilac Cottage was a hive of activity. The table was covered with freshly-baked pies, cakes and scones. Mandy's gran was just lifting another sponge cake out of the oven, while Mandy's grandad was cutting the milk cartons off some of the bird feeders they'd made.

"Gosh! You have been busy," Mandy said. "Look, Grandad." She opened her school bag

and pulled out a pile of papers. "Dad let me use the surgery computer last night, and I found some recipes for dog and cat treats on the internet."

"That sounds interesting, love." Grandad took the papers and flicked through them. "Peanut-butter bones. Cat Munchies. Mini Cakes. Doggie Doughnuts." He winked at Mandy and James. "Looks like the animals of Welford are going to be eating better than we are!"

"I'm going to put all the things I've made into the freezer," Gran told them, putting down her oven gloves. "So you'll have plenty of room to make your animal treats."

Mandy and James ran to put their aprons on, while Grandad started collecting together the ingredients for the peanut-butter bones.

"We won't be able to come tomorrow morning, Gran," Mandy said. "We're going over to Oliver's to help him when the hamsters arrive," she explained. "But we'll come here straight afterwards."

"Why don't you come for lunch?" Gran

suggested, opening the freezer.

"Oh, yum!" said James happily. "That'd be great, Mrs Hope."

"And bring Oliver along," Gran went on. "If he's not too busy with his hamster camp, that is!"

"I wonder which hamster will arrive first," Mandy said eagerly. It was the following morning. She, James and Oliver were sitting in the Morgans' living-room, waiting for the guests to arrive.

"Let's hope they don't all come at once!" Oliver replied, putting his *Hamster Camp* folder on the coffee table. Mandy was very impressed with how organised Oliver was. He'd divided the folder into sections, one for each hamster, and there was a whole page to note down important things like any special diet that was required. There was also space for emergency phone numbers, in case Oliver had to contact the owners.

"Here's Mary," James said suddenly, as a figure appeared at the end of the path.

"And Frisky," Mandy added, looking out of the window to see Mary carrying a large cage.

Oliver jumped up. "My very first guest!" he said excitedly. Then he frowned. "Tammy, stop that!" Tammy had sneaked the folder off the table and was about to start drawing in it with her crayons. Quickly, Mandy rescued the folder, and they all hurried to open the door.

Mary smiled at them, holding up the cage. "You must be Oliver," she said. "Meet Frisky."

"Oh, Frisky's a Russian hamster," Oliver said with delight as Frisky popped his golden head out of his pile of fleecy bedding. "I've never seen one of those before."

Frisky stared at Oliver, Mandy and James with his bright, dark eyes for a moment, and then burrowed down into his bedding again.

"He doesn't have a special diet or anything," Mary told them. "But you will keep him nice and warm, won't you?"

"Of course I will," Oliver promised. "Would you like to come and see where I'll be keeping him?"

Mary nodded, so they took her upstairs to

the loft. She was very impressed. "It's a lovely place," she said, looking around at the clean shelves and the neat stack of hamster books on the desk. The hamster-run, made from taped-together cardboard boxes, lay in the middle of the floor. "This really *will* be a holiday for Frisky!"

"He's going to be fine," Mandy said, as she carefully put Frisky's cage on one of the shelves.

After Frisky, the other hamsters started arriving quickly. Daniel Burton was next with Milly, a ginger hamster, and Mungo, who was black. Then Billy from the lady in Walton. He was golden with patches of white. Pinky followed soon after – she was the same colour as Billy.

"Maybe we should put labels on the cages," Mandy suggested. "Then we won't get them mixed up."

Oliver and James thought that was a very good idea. Oliver opened one of the desk drawers and took out a sheet of white card and some felt-tip pens. They'd just started writing out the hamster names when the doorbell rang again. Mandy led the way as they ran downstairs.

A young couple stood on the doorstep. The man was holding a large plastic tank in his arms. Mandy blinked. She was expecting a hamster cage. What was going on?

"Er – are you here for the hamster camp?" Oliver asked, looking as puzzled as Mandy and James.

The man nodded. "I'm Jack Beasley, and this is my wife, Miriam." He smiled. "And this is our hamster, Herbert."

Mandy, James and Oliver stared into the tank. A little face peeped back at them. The hamster was golden-orange in colour with a white tummy and lovely white, furry eyebrows.

Mandy gave a little gasp. "Oh, it's a Roborovski hamster!" she said. "Did I say that right? I've never seen one before."

Miriam Beasley nodded. "Yes, Herbert's really special," she said proudly. "There aren't many hamsters like him in the country."

"Why is he in a tank and not a cage?" James asked, looking fascinated.

"These kind of hamsters are really active," Mr Beasley explained. "Sometimes they can squeeze through the bars of an ordinary cage."

"And when they get away, they're really fast," Mrs Beasley added. "And hard to catch!"

"They're quite difficult to handle too, aren't they?" Mandy said, remembering what she'd read.

Mrs Beasley nodded. "Herbert's not too bad. He won't nip you, but he'll probably try to get away!" She frowned. "This is the first time we've ever left him with anyone. I hope he'll be all right." She opened her handbag and took out a list. "These are the foods he likes, and the ones he doesn't. Oh, and don't put his cage in bright sunlight."

Mandy couldn't help smiling. Herbert was obviously a *very* special pet!

"Don't worry, I'll look after him properly," Oliver said. "Would you like to come up and see where Herbert will be staying?"

Herbert's tank took up most of one shelf in the loft, but Mandy was glad to see that there was still some space left for the other hamsters. Barney arrived a few moments after the Beasleys had left, and that just left the McDonald family, who were coming with their five babies.

"Here they are," James said, as a car drew up outside the house.

A woman climbed out of the car, followed by identical twin boys, one of whom was carrying a big cage. Mandy and James crowded round Oliver as he opened the door. They couldn't wait to see the baby hamsters.

"Hello, I'm Mrs McDonald," the woman announced with a friendly smile. "These are my sons, Angus and Robert."

Mandy peered eagerly into the cage. The baby hamsters were all curled up together in a corner, a tangle of different colours. They looked really sweet.

"We'd better tell you which is which," said Angus, who was carrying the cage. "That tortoiseshell one's called Charlie, the ginger one is Toffee, the grey-and-white one's Lulu—'

"The ginger-and-white one's Biscuit, and the

grey one is Peanut," Robert interrupted his brother.

"Charlie, Toffee and Lulu are pretty lively," Angus went on. "We call them the Three Musketeers! They can be a bit naughty—'

"So you'll have to keep an eye on them," Robert finished off. Mandy wondered if they always talked like that!

As if they'd heard their names, Charlie, Toffee and Lulu scrambled their way out from the corner and started scampering about. Mandy grinned. What with Herbert and the Three Musketeers, it looked like they were in for a really interesting time . . .

"That was a great lunch, Mrs Hope." Oliver patted his stomach. "Thanks very much."

"You're welcome," Mandy's gran replied.

"Oliver's going to stay and help us with the baking, Gran," Mandy said. "Is that OK?"

Her gran nodded. "Of course," she said. "But doesn't Oliver want to get back to his hamster camp?"

"They'll be fine on their own for a bit,"

Oliver replied. "We got them settled in, and now they're all asleep." Then he frowned. "But maybe I *will* just pop back and check."

"You can always ring home," Grandad suggested. "Use our phone."

Oliver looked relieved. "Thanks, Mr Hope," he said. "I'll do it later. I'm a bit worried about my sister, Tammy. Even though I locked the loft door, she might find a way to get in there."

"Oh, I'm sure she won't," said Mandy's gran.

"You don't know Tammy!" Oliver muttered.

"Gran, can we use the animal-shaped cutters today?" Mandy asked.

"Of course! How about making gingerbread animals?" her gran suggested. "It would be a change from gingerbread men!"

"Great idea!" said Mandy. Beside her, James and Oliver beamed and nodded enthusiastically.

Mandy's gran helped them to measure out the ingredients for the gingerbread, and James and Oliver mixed them together in a big china bowl. Mandy couldn't wait to start cutting the animal shapes out of the soft, doughy mixture. That was the best bit. Once that was done, they laid their animal shapes on baking trays and put them in the oven to cook.

"Mr Hope, could I use the phone now, please?" Oliver asked.

Grandad nodded, and Oliver hurried out into the hall.

"I hope everything's OK," Mandy said to James.

"Yes, especially with five babies, and Herbert the rare hamster!" James agreed. "I'd never even heard of a Rob—' He paused, looking at Mandy for help.

"Roborovski," Mandy finished, laughing.

Oliver came back into the kitchen, looking relieved. "Mum says all the hamsters are still asleep," he said. "Everything's fine."

"Good," Mandy replied. She just hoped that the rest of the hamster camp went smoothly.

5

A Hamster Crisis

"I'll get it, Mum!" Mandy called, skipping down the stairs. It was quite early the following morning, and the phone in the Hopes' cottage was ringing. As she reached the bottom step, Mandy frowned and glanced at the hall clock. It really *was* early for anyone to be calling. Maybe it was an animal emergency, she thought, lifting the receiver. If the surgery was closed, then people always rang the Hopes' private number.

"Mandy?" It was Oliver. "Oh, Mandy, you'll never guess what's happened!"

"What?" Mandy asked, her heart sinking. Oliver sounded really upset.

"I left the loft door open this morning while I was feeding the hamsters," Oliver said miserably. "Tammy got in and let some of

them out of their cages. And now I can't find four of them."

"Oh no!" Mandy gasped, her hand flying to her mouth. "Which ones?"

"Herbert." Oliver gulped. "And three of the babies. Charlie, Toffee and Lulu."

Mandy groaned. Herbert, the rare hamster, and the Three Musketeers were missing. This was awful. "I'll come over and help you look," she said quickly. She and James had arranged to go to Lilac Cottage that morning, but finding the hamsters was more important. "I'll just ring Gran to tell her we won't be coming until later and then I'll ask Dad to bring me over."

"Oh, thanks, Mandy," Oliver said gratefully. "I just called James, and he's already on his way."

Mandy rang off and ran into the kitchen. Her mum and dad were getting breakfast.

"Dad, Oliver's little sister has let some of the hamsters out, and Oliver can't find them," Mandy said breathlessly. "Could you take me over there so that I can help him look?"

"What, now?" Mr Hope raised his eyebrows. Mandy nodded. "Please, Dad."

"Which hamsters are they?" Emily Hope asked, looking concerned.

"Herbert and three of the babies," Mandy replied, grabbing her coat.

"Oh dear, isn't Herbert the Roborovski hamster you were telling us about last night?" Mandy's mum frowned. "They're very fast. You might find it difficult to catch him."

"Be careful how you handle Herbert, Mandy," her dad warned her, as they went out to the car. "Roborovski hamsters are lovely to look at, but they're not keen on being picked up."

"OK," Mandy said, as Mr Hope started the engine.

Mrs Morgan answered the door when Mandy rang the bell. She looked worried. "Oliver and James are in the loft," she said. "You'd better go straight up."

"Have they found any of the missing hamsters yet?" Mandy asked anxiously.

Mrs Morgan shook her head. "No," she

replied. "I'd come and help too, but I think I'd better keep an eye on Tammy!" She pointed into the living-room, where Oliver's little sister was sitting in front of the TV, watching cartoons.

Mandy ran up the stairs and into the loft. James and Oliver were crawling around on the floor, both of them red in the face.

"Any luck?" Mandy asked.

"No, all four of them are still missing," Oliver groaned.

"Maybe we should just stand still and listen," Mandy suggested. "We might hear something."

They all stayed quietly where they were and listened hard. At first, the only thing they could hear was the rain, which had just started pitter-pattering down on the roof.

Then Mandy's face lit up. "I can hear something scratching," she whispered.

"So can I," James hissed. "Over there, in the hamster run!"

The hamster run was laid out in the middle of the floor. Mandy, James and Oliver had also put in things like cardboard tubes from toilet rolls for the hamsters to run through. Carefully, Mandy picked up one of the cardboard tubes – and Charlie ran out on to her hand.

"Thank goodness!" Oliver breathed. "Now, what about the others?"

"There's one!" James cried, as a flash of grey-and-white scurried across the room. Next moment, Oliver discovered Lulu behind the bookcase.

"Just Toffee and Herbert left," Mandy said, looking around.

They searched the loft carefully, but couldn't find either of the two remaining hamsters. It wasn't until James looked under the desk for the third time that he spotted Herbert crouched behind one of the legs, next to the wall. Oliver knelt down beside James and stretched out his hand.

"No, don't, Oliver," Mandy said quickly. "He'll run off." She thought for a minute. "Have you got that list the Beasleys gave us?"

Oliver nodded. His folder was lying on the desk, and he took the list out and gave it to Mandy.

She glanced down it quickly. "It says here that Herbert loves apples." She looked up at the others and grinned. "I think *that's* the way to catch him."

Oliver ran downstairs and came back with a small piece of apple. Mandy put it on the floor just in front of the desk, and they stepped back. A moment later, Herbert trotted over to the apple, sniffed it, and began stuffing it happily into his cheek pouches. Mandy scooped him up quickly, keeping a firm hold on him, even though he paddled his tiny feet against her hand. Soon Herbert was safely back in his plastic tank.

"Just Toffee now," Oliver said.

"But we've looked *everywhere*," James protested. "Where can Toffee possibly be?"

Mandy turned slowly on her heel, staring round the room. Then she began to laugh. A huge ginger teddy bear sat on the floor near the bed. There, snuggled in the teddy bear's furry lap, was a little ginger hamster. He was almost invisible.

"That was a great disguise, Toffee!" Mandy

laughed, gently rescuing the hamster from his comfy bed. Toffee sat quite happily in Mandy's hand, twitching his little pink nose. "We nearly didn't spot you there."

"That's it, we've got them all." Oliver looked very relieved, as he returned Toffee to his brothers and sisters. "Thanks, you two!"

"That's OK." Mandy grinned. "But I think you'd better make sure you keep Tammy out of the loft from now on!"

"Well, thank goodness you found them all," Mandy's gran said, as she popped another tray of peanut-butter bones into the oven to bake. "Poor Oliver must have been very upset."

"He was," Mandy replied. She and James were mixing together the ingredients for some doggie doughnuts. After helping Oliver to catch the hamsters, they'd gone back to Animal Ark for lunch, and then on to Lilac Cottage. Oliver hadn't come to help with the baking this time, as the Morgans had gone Christmas shopping in York.

"Let's hope nothing else goes wrong,"

Grandad said, handing Mandy some flour. James put the bowl on the scales, ready to weigh it out.

Gran took off her oven gloves and put them on the side. "Goodness me, listen to the rain," she said. "Is your mum coming to collect you, Mandy? You'll get soaked otherwise."

"Yes, she is," Mandy replied. The rain was much heavier now, and it was pounding on the cottage roof.

"Oh, that's good," said Gran.

Mandy was about to tackle her gran again about the identity of the special guests at the Christmas Fair, but thought better of it when she looked around her. Gran had enough on her plate! Mandy watched as she began wrapping up all the things they'd baked that afternoon.

"I'd better get these put away," said Gran. "My freezer's going to be full at this rate!"

"Better make sure you don't mix things up, Dorothy," Grandad teased, "or we'll be selling peanut-butter bones to people, and gingerbread biscuits for their dogs!"

Mandy and James laughed.

"I'll have you know that I've labelled everything clearly, Tom Hope!" Gran said, wagging her finger at him. Just then there was a knock at the door. "Would you see who that is, Mandy?"

Mandy went to open the door. She was surprised to see Oliver and his mum on the doorstep, huddled under a huge umbrella.

"Come in." Mandy opened the door wider, wondering what on earth had happened. Both Oliver and Mrs Morgan looked damp and worried.

"You'll never guess what's happened," Oliver said unhappily. "We've just got home, and the loft is leaking. It's full of rainwater, Mandy!"

Mandy's eyes opened wide. "Are the hamsters all right?" she gasped.

"The hamsters are fine," Mrs Morgan said. "We've moved them to the dining-room for the moment. It's the skylights that are the problem. They're not watertight. And the builders can't come back to fix them until after Christmas."

Mandy's heart began to pound. "So what will happen to the hamsters?" she asked.

"I can't keep them in the loft any more," Oliver said. "It's too damp. And I can't keep them in the dining-room. The cages take up too much space, and some of them are on the floor which is really draughty." He looked miserably at Mandy. "What am I going to do?"

6

New Homes Required

"We need a new hamster camp!" Mandy was feeling very anxious. Oliver and his mum had joined them by the fire in the living-room at Lilac Cottage. Gran had supplied them with freshly-baked scones. "How long do you think they can stay in the dining-room?"

"Well, the door doesn't lock," Oliver

explained. "So Tammy could get in at any time."

"And we've got relatives coming for Christmas lunch," Mrs Morgan added. "I don't think we can have twelve hamsters in there too!"

"Don't you have a spare bedroom?" Mandy asked.

"Yes, but the floorboards have been taken up," Oliver replied. "They've got to be replaced, but the builders aren't coming back till after Christmas. And my bedroom's full of boxes we haven't unpacked yet."

"What about phoning the owners?" Grandad suggested. "Maybe some of them could make other arrangements."

"We did phone them, but most of them are staying with people miles away," Oliver said gloomily. "They've all asked me to keep on looking after their hamsters – somehow." He looked hopefully at Mandy. "I was wondering . . . what about Animal Ark? Would you have room for them there?"

Mandy frowned. "I'm not sure," she began,

just as there was a knock at the door.

"That'll be your mum, Mandy," Gran said. "I'll go and fetch another cup."

Grandad went to answer the door and came back very shortly, followed by Emily Hope. She was shaking the raindrops from her long, red hair. "Oh, dear," she said, glancing at the Morgans. "I hear you've had a problem with the hamster camp. Tom's just been telling me about it."

"I was asking Mandy if there was room for the hamsters to move to Animal Ark," Oliver said eagerly.

Mrs Hope shook her head. "I'm sorry, Oliver," she said. "But we have to keep the surgery clear in case we get any emergency cases."

"I can't have them at my place either," James said. "We're going to my gran's on the day after Boxing Day, and we're not coming back for a week."

"Maybe I could look after a few of them," Mandy said eagerly. "I could keep them in my bedroom."

"Oh, Mandy, there's hardly enough room for all your animal books, let alone a dozen hamster cages," her mum pointed out gently.

"We could take Frisky, I suppose." Gran looked over at Grandad.

"But you're so busy with the fair," Oliver said. "And, anyway, it would be easier if I could keep them all together, because I'm still going to have to feed them and clean them out."

Mandy's mum looked at Gran. "And aren't you going to visit friends on Boxing Day?"

Gran nodded.

"What about Maggie Trigg?" Grandad suggested. "She lives on her own, except for Holly, and she's got plenty of room." Mandy and James had made friends with Mrs Trigg's grandson, Max, when he'd come to stay in Welford with his dog, Sandy. Then Mrs Trigg adopted a puppy of her own, called Holly.

"Mrs Trigg and Holly are going to stay with Max's mum and dad over Christmas," Mandy replied. She frowned, thinking hard. It seemed that almost *everyone* she knew in the village was going away at some point over Christmas, even if it was only for a day or two.

"Hey, what about Libby Masters?" James said eagerly. Libby and her family lived at Blackheath Farm. "They've got a barn. That would be big enough for all the hamsters. And they wouldn't be going away, because they've got all the hens to look after."

But Mandy shook her head. "A barn would be too cold, James," she pointed out.

"And it would be a long way for Oliver to go every day to feed them and clean them out,"

Gran added. "It would be the same problem if we asked Betty Hilder at the animal sanctuary. That's right over the other side of Welford."

"The animal sanctuary is full to bursting at the moment anyway," Mrs Hope said. "I'm sure Betty wouldn't have any room."

Oliver sighed. "It looks like I'm going to have to split them up after all," he said. "How on earth am I going to find enough people to look after them, Mandy?"

"Don't worry," Mandy said in a determined voice. "James and I will help you. We'll start ringing round all our friends from school as soon as we get home."

"Thanks, Mandy," Oliver said gratefully.

Mandy managed to smile, even though she was secretly feeling very worried. Finding temporary homes for twelve hamsters was a big responsibility. And someone would have to be prepared to take on all five babies together, because they couldn't split them up. It wasn't going to be easy.

7

A Brilliant Idea

"OK, Richard." Mandy sighed. "Thanks anyway." She put the phone down, and crossed another name off her list.

It was the following morning. As she had promised, Mandy was ringing round some of her friends to find out if any of them could take a hamster. But she wasn't having any luck. Everyone she'd tried so far was going away at some point during the holiday.

Mandy sucked the end of her pen and thought hard. Maybe they would have to keep moving the hamsters around. Richard Tanner had offered to look after one of them until Boxing Day, when he and his family were going to visit his aunt. Maybe then someone else could take over. But it wasn't ideal. Mandy didn't like the idea of the hamsters being moved around all over the place.

Mandy looked at the next name on her list. Pam Stanton. She was about to pick up the phone when it rang, making her jump.

It was Oliver. "Any luck, Mandy?" he asked eagerly.

"Not yet," Mandy said. "But I've still got lots of other people to try."

"Oh dear." Oliver sounded very glum. "Mum says I've got to move them out of the dining-room soon, because Dad wants to finish decorating it before Christmas Day."

"What are you going to do?" Mandy asked.

"Put them in the living-room, I suppose," Oliver said. "But I'll have to watch Tammy all the time. She's just itching to let them out."

"Shall I pop over and help you move them?" Mandy offered.

"Oh, thanks, Mandy." Oliver sounded really grateful. "But isn't it the Christmas Fair tomorrow? You must be very busy."

"Well, James and I are going to Lilac Cottage later," Mandy replied. "But I can come and help you first."

"OK. Thanks." And Oliver rang off.

Mandy felt really sorry for him. He obviously hated the idea of letting all the hamster owners down.

Mandy went into the kitchen, and then through the door to the surgery. Her dad had gone to a choir practice at St Luke's Church in Welford, while Mrs Hope was taking morning surgery. There weren't any patients in at the moment, and Emily Hope was in her consulting-room writing up some notes in her files.

"No luck with the hamsters yet?" Mrs Hope asked.

Mandy shook her head. "Mum, can I go over

to the Morgans' house?" she asked. "Oliver needs some help to move the hamsters."

Her mum nodded. "Yes, but you'll have to walk, I'm afraid," she said. "I've still got a few patients left to see. It's a good job we're not busy this morning," she went on, 'because Jean's at the choir practice too." Jean Knox was the Animal Ark receptionist.

"Bye then, Mum." Mandy went to get her coat.

A few moments later, she was on her way to James's house. The rain had stopped now, but all the trees were still dripping with raindrops and the sky was grey. Mandy hurried quickly up the Hunters' path. She and James had arranged to meet later that morning to go to Lilac Cottage. He wasn't expecting her now, and he might not be in.

Mandy rang the doorbell. At once she heard Blackie barking madly, and then James shouting, 'Blackie! Give me that!"

Mandy grinned to herself. What was Blackie up to now?

James opened the door, looking rather red

in the face. Behind him, Blackie wagged his tail and then launched himself at Mandy. He was trailing a long piece of silver tinsel in his mouth.

"He pulled it off the tree and he won't give it back," James explained breathlessly. "Bad boy, Blackie!" Then he looked puzzled. "It's not time to go to Lilac Cottage yet, is it?"

"No, I'm early." Quickly Mandy explained about Oliver having to move the hamsters. "I'm going over to help him. Can you come?"

"OK," said James, reaching for his coat. Blackie immediately dropped the tinsel and began barking excitedly.

"Sorry, Blackie." Mandy patted the puppy's sleek black head. "You can't come – you'll frighten the hamsters!"

"Did you find anyone who can help us?" James asked as he and Mandy set off through Welford, leaving a disappointed Blackie behind.

Mandy shook her head. "No," she said glumly. "Everyone I've spoken to seems to be going away, or they're too busy."

"I had the same problem," James replied. "It looks like Oliver might have to keep the hamsters after all."

"It's really difficult for him though," Mandy pointed out. "He's terrified that Tammy's going to let them out again, and that they'll get lost all over the house. Also, the loft is perfect. It's the warmest room in the house."

"Come on, let's cut through the churchyard," James suggested, pushing his glasses up on his nose. "It's quicker that way, and I'm freezing!"

Mandy pushed open the low wooden gate and they walked into St Luke's churchyard. The church was built of old grey stone, and it had a tall steeple and beautiful stained-glass windows. The heavy wooden doors stood open, and Mandy and James could hear singing inside.

"It's the choir practising," Mandy said. They stopped and listened for a moment as the choir began to sing *O Come All Ye Faithful*.

"Your dad must be busy over Christmas with all the church services," James remarked, as they walked past the church. "Aren't they going carol-singing round the village tomorrow night, as well?"

Mandy nodded. "Yes. There's a service on Christmas Eve and Christmas Day *and* on Boxing Day this year, because it's on a Sunday. And then after Christmas the choir are singing at some old peoples' homes in Walton and Welford."

"No wonder you're not going away anywhere over Christmas!" James said.

"Yes," said Mandy. "What with Animal Ark *and* the choir—' She stopped – so suddenly that James almost bumped into her. "That's it." Mandy started smiling. "I've got it!"

"Got what?" James asked, puzzled.

"The choir!" Mandy beamed at James. "None of *them* will be going away, will they? Maybe some of the people in the choir could look after Oliver's hamsters."

James gave a gasp of delight. "Mandy, you're a genius!" he cried. "That's a *brilliant* idea!"

8

Choir to the Rescue!

"Quiet, James," Mandy whispered, as they tiptoed into the church. "We'll have to wait till choir practice is over." They sat down in a pew at the back, and waited.

The choir were now singing "Once in Royal David's City". They were standing in the choir stalls at the front of the church, and so far no one had noticed Mandy and James.

"Well done," said Mr Raymond, the churchwarden, who was in charge of the choir. "Now let's try 'Hark the Herald Angels Sing'."

Mandy and James sat patiently as the singing began again. It was quite chilly inside the old stone building, but Mandy hardly noticed. She was too busy worrying about the hamsters. Would they manage to find enough members of the choir to take a special guest home for Christmas?

Mandy counted up the members of the choir. There were fourteen of them, including her dad. Oliver needed eight volunteers, because the babies would have to stay together. Mandy bit her lip. It still sounded an awful lot. Only fourteen people to ask, well, thirteen really, if you didn't count her dad. Would there be enough volunteers?

Mandy craned her neck round the end of the pew and looked down the aisle at the choir. There was Amy Fenton, who was in James's class at school. Amy loved animals. She had a white mouse called Minnie and a baby rabbit called Tulip. Mandy was sure Amy would give

a home to one of the hamsters, if her parents
let her. Then there was Jean Knox, the
receptionist at Animal Ark. She loved animals
too. And there was Mrs Ponsonby, singing
loudly. She lived at Bleakfell Hall and she had
a spoilt Pekinese dog called Pandora. Mrs
Ponsonby was the bossiest person in Welford!
But she might help out.

Mandy began to feel a bit more hopeful. There was Mrs Mcfarlane from the Post Office, as well as Kathy, who was a friend of Gran and Grandad's. And then were several other people from the village whom Mandy didn't know so well, but one of them might volunteer to take a hamster.

As the carol finished James nudged Mandy. "There are quite a few people in the choir who like animals," he whispered hopefully. Mandy smiled. James had obviously been thinking exactly the same thing as her! 'Do you think we'll get enough people?" he asked.

"I hope so," Mandy whispered back, as the choir launched into "O Little Town of Bethlehem". She glanced at her watch, hoping the practice wouldn't go on for much longer. Oliver would be wondering where they were.

"Hello, you two," said a friendly voice behind them. "Are you waiting to see me?"

Mandy and James turned round. Reverend Hadcroft was standing in the aisle, smiling at them.

"Hello, Reverend Hadcroft," Mandy said.

"Actually, we were waiting to see your choir."

"The choir?" Reverend Hadcroft ran a hand through his dark curly hair, looking puzzled.

Quickly Mandy explained why they were there.

Reverend Hadcroft nodded. "Oh, yes, I heard about the hamster camp," he said. "I thought it was a marvellous idea. What a shame about the flooding."

"Yes, it is!" Mandy nodded. "We've been trying to find temporary homes for all the hamsters. But lots of people are away. We were hoping that the choir might be able to help," she finished eagerly.

"There aren't many people in the village who are going to be here every day over Christmas," James explained. "But everyone in the choir will be."

Reverend Hadcroft smiled. "I think it's an excellent idea," he said. "I'm going to be here myself because of the services, and I've got plenty of room at the vicarage. Would you like me to take a hamster?"

"Really?" Mandy gasped, delighted. She

glanced at James. "Would you mind taking five hamsters — but they're babies, so they're all in one cage," she added hurriedly.

"Certainly," Reverend Hadcroft agreed. "And it looks like the choir have just finished, so why don't you come along and ask them?"

The choir had put down their hymn sheets, and Mr Raymond was giving them instructions about tomorrow's carol-singing tour of Welford. "Now, remember, we meet here at the church at 6.30 sharp," he said. "And don't forget your lanterns."

Everyone in the choir stared at Mandy and James as they walked towards the front of the church with Reverend Hadcroft. Mandy grinned when she saw the puzzled look on her dad's face. He was probably wondering what they were up to.

"Can I have your attention, everyone?" Reverend Hadcroft held up his hand. "Before you go, Mandy and James have something to ask you."

Feeling a bit nervous, Mandy stepped forward and explained what had happened with Oliver's hamster camp. "And so we really need seven people to take just one hamster home each, now that Reverend Hadcroft has offered to have the babies." She stopped and looked around hopefully. "Would anyone like a hamster for Christmas?"

There was silence for a few seconds.

"I'll have one," Amy piped up eagerly. "I'm sure Mum and Dad would let me."

"That'd be great," James said, his eyes shining behind his glasses.

"Hmm." Mrs Ponsonby frowned and folded her arms. "Aren't hamsters a lot of work, Mandy?"

"No, not at all," Mandy said quickly. "And anyway, Oliver will come round regularly to clean them out. He'll come and feed them every day as well, if you're too busy."

Mrs Ponsonby didn't look very convinced.

"I'll take one, Mandy," Jean Knox said kindly. "How about you, Kathy?"

Kathy nodded. "Of course I will," she said. "I'm sure LaLa won't mind too much!" LaLa was Kathy's deaf Siamese cat.

"Oh, thank you," Mandy gasped. Now they needed just four more people.

"Go on then, Mandy." Mrs McFarlane smiled. "I'll have one. I'm very busy though. I've got a lot of people coming to stay for Christmas, so I'll really need Oliver to help me out."

"I'll help too," Mandy promised, her heart thumping with excitement.

Mr Raymond was stroking his chin thoughtfully. "I suppose I could take a couple, if they're not too much trouble," he said slowly. "Put me down for two, Mandy."

Mandy and James looked at each other in delight.

"Of course, it's just the right time of the year to take in a homeless guest," Reverend Hadcroft put in, glancing at Mrs Ponsonby. "It *is* the season of goodwill to all men, after all. And I think that includes hamsters!"

Mrs Ponsonby nodded. "Well, I suppose I might be able to help you out, Mandy," she said graciously. "I do have plenty of room at Bleakfell Hall, after all."

"Thanks, Mrs Ponsonby," Mandy said gratefully. "We've got a very rare hamster for you." Mandy was sure that Herbert would be very well looked after at Bleakfell Hall, and would probably end up being as spoilt as Pandora!

Mrs Ponsonby looked pleased and interested. "You must tell me all about him," she said.

"Don't worry, Mrs Posonby," said Mandy with a grin. "We've got lists and lists of what he likes to eat, and where he likes to sleep!"

"We did it, Mandy!" James said, as the choir began to leave. "We found homes for all the hamsters."

"I know, and I can't wait to tell Oliver," Mandy replied.

Mandy's dad came over to them. "You two!" he said, shaking his head. "What will you think of next?"

"It was Mandy's idea, Dad," James told him.

"Yes, and it's a very good one," Adam Hope said. "You've made sure that twelve hamsters are going to be safe and warm and well-looked after this Christmas."

★ ★ ★

"Cheer up, Oliver," Mandy said, as their friend opened the door of the Morgans' house. Oliver looked pale and very miserable. "We've got some great news for you."

"Oh, have you found homes for some of the hamsters?" Oliver asked, his face brightening.

"Not just some of them." James beamed. "*All* of them!"

"What?" Oliver gasped.

Quickly Mandy explained.

Oliver let out a long sigh of relief. "That's great," he said. "When can they go to their new homes?"

"We've arranged for them to be picked up after the carol-singing tomorrow night," Mandy explained. "And Dad thinks it's better if the volunteers collect them from Animal Ark, so that he and Mum can talk to anyone who might need some advice."

"Mr Hope's going to come and collect the hamsters tomorrow morning, before the Christmas Fair," James added.

Oliver beamed at them. "Thank goodness,"

he said, leading the way into the dining-room. "I was so worried about what was going to happen—' He broke off in alarm. "Oh no! *Tammy!*"

Oliver's sister was standing on a chair, her hand inside Herbert's plastic tank, which was on the table.

Oliver rushed across the room and lifted her down from the chair. "She keeps sneaking in and trying to get the hamsters out," Oliver said, as Tammy toddled off. "I'll be glad when they've gone to their new homes, although I'm really going to miss them."

"You'll still see a lot of them," Mandy pointed out. She bent down and wrinkled her nose at Toffee, who was peering up at her from the babies' cage. "And they'll be well looked after."

"Hello, Mandy, hello, James." Mrs Morgan came in, carrying Tammy. They were followed by Mr Morgan, who had a paintbrush in his hand. "Did I hear you say you'd found homes for all the hamsters?"

Mandy and James nodded.

"What a relief!" Mrs Morgan exclaimed.

"Maybe now we can all relax and enjoy Christmas."

"And I can get on with decorating the dining-room," Mr Morgan said.

"Will you help me to move the hamsters into the living-room?" Oliver asked Mandy and James. "Then I'll come over to Lilac Cottage with you."

"And don't worry about Tammy," Mrs Morgan added, keeping a firm grip on the little girl. "I'll keep a close eye on her." She carried Tammy out to the kichen.

"Thanks again," Oliver said gratefully to Mandy and James, as they all picked up a cage each. "I don't know what I'd have done without you."

"That's OK," Mandy replied. The hamsters were going to be safe and well, and that was all that mattered.

"Well, that's wonderful news," Mandy's gran declared, as she carefully spread chocolate icing on to a sponge cake. "I'm so glad you managed to find homes for the poor things."

"So are we, Gran," Mandy replied. She and Oliver were cutting up bits of apple, banana, grapes, carrots and cucumber, and sealing them tightly in paper bags. Meanwhile, James was writing *Hamster Treats* and *Rabbit Treats* on sticky labels, to put on the bags. "We were getting really worried."

"I'm surprised Mrs Ponsonby agreed to take one of the hamsters," Grandad said. "Isn't she worried Pandora might be jealous?"

"I think Mrs Ponsonby will look after Herbert really well." Mandy grinned. "We'll just have to be careful she doesn't give him too much food, that's all." Pandora was quite a plump Peke, because of all the treats her owner gave her.

"I can't wait for the fair tomorrow," James said eagerly. He glanced at Mandy. With all the hamster drama, they had hardly had time to think about the big secret.

Mandy looked longingly at her gran. "*Now* will you tell us who the special guests are going to be?" she begged.

Gran's eyes twinkled mischeviously. "I can't give anything away, I'm afraid. But you haven't got long to wait now!"

"Have you finished your special Christmas cake yet, Mrs Hope?" James asked. "The one for the competition?"

Gran nodded. "You can have a peep at it, if you like." She disappeared into the larder, and came back carrying the most enormous Christmas cake that Mandy had ever seen. The top was decorated with white icing to look like snow, and there was a woodland scene with little trees and animals, all made out of marzipan. Deer, rabbits, a fox and a black dog stood around, looking very festive. There were even some tiny animal footprints in the icing sugar.

"Wow!" James gasped. "Whoever wins that is going to be really lucky!"

"Oh, Gran." Mandy began to laugh, as she spotted something else. "You've even got Harold there." She pointed at a little brown marzipan hedgehog, tucked away behind one of the trees.

"Yes, I know Harold is hibernating by now, but I wanted to put him in," Gran told her. Harold was the hedgehog who lived in Mary's garden. "So what do you think?"

"I think it's perfect!" Mandy smiled, gazing at the cake. "I wonder who's going to win it?"

9

Gran's Secret

"Mandy, have you put out all the animal treats?" Gran asked, bustling around behind the large stall. "The fair's going to be starting in a few minutes."

"I think so, Gran." Mandy stopped to take a rest, and pushed her hair out of her eyes. She, Oliver and James had been helping Gran and Grandad set up the stall in the church hall.

The time had flown! Soon they would find out what the surprise was.

"The stall looks great," James said, looking proudly at their handiwork. "Doesn't it, Mandy?"

Mandy nodded. All their hard work had definitely been worth it. The stall looked wonderful. A snowy-white tablecloth covered the long trestle table, and James and Oliver had wound red and green tinsel round the table legs. All the things that Mandy's gran had baked were stacked neatly at one end of the table, with the animal treats at the other. Mandy and James had made a big sign which read *Your Pet Deserves a Merry Christmas too! Why not buy them some of our special home-made PET TREATS?* They'd hung it on the wall behind the stall. Next to the big table was a much smaller one, which held Gran's Christmas cake for the competition.

"What do you have to do to win the cake?" Oliver asked curiously.

"You'll find out when our two special guests arrive," Gran said with a grin.

"And what's that for?" Oliver looked even more puzzled as he pointed to a small wooden pen. Grandad had set it up next to the other tables.

"Wait and see!" Gran said mysteriously. "Oh, look, they're opening the doors now."

People flocked into the hall and began to mill around the stalls. There were lots of lovely things for sale – homemade jam, pottery, candles, plants, handmade sweaters, and Christmas decorations.

"This looks wonderful," Emily Hope said warmly, as she came over to the stall. "What a fantastic range of animal treats!"

"And they're all homemade," James pointed out proudly.

"Where's Dad?" Mandy asked her mum.

Mrs Hope shrugged. "Oh, he's around somewhere."

"Now don't sell anything yet," Gran warned them, as Mandy, James and Oliver stationed themselves behind the animal treats. Oliver was holding a plastic tub to collect money in. "We have to wait for the official opening."

"Who's opening the fair, Gran?" Mandy asked.

Her gran's eyes twinkled. "Someone you know very well indeed!" she said. "Ah, here they are."

Mrs Ponsonby, who was the chairperson of the Welford Women's Institute, swept importantly through the doors into the hall. She was wearing one of her famous hats, an exotic purple creation with fake yellow flowers stuck on one side, and a matching purple coat. She was followed by the Reverend Hadcroft, and . . .

"It's Dad!" Mandy exclaimed. "Is *he* opening the fair, Gran?"

"It looks like it!" Her gran smiled, as Mr Hope followed Mrs Ponsonby and Reverend Hadcroft onto the stage.

"A very warm welcome to you all," said Mrs Ponsonby, smiling round at everyone. "We're very pleased to see so many of you at our Christmas Fair, and we'd like to thank Reverend Hadcroft for lending us the church hall. As the fair is in aid of the RSPCA, we thought we'd ask our local vet, Adam Hope, to say a few words to declare the fair officially open."

There was a ripple of applause as Mandy's dad stepped to the front of the stage. "You all know that the RSPCA is a very worthy cause," he began, 'so please, spend lots of money!"

Everyone laughed.

"And if any of you have pets," Mr Hope went on, 'do visit the animal treats stall over there in the corner, where my daughter Mandy

and her friends will be delighted to serve you."

Mandy, James and Oliver grinned as everyone turned round to look at them.

"I now declare this fair open!" Mandy's dad said, and everyone applauded.

"I'm going to donate my money from the hamster camp to the RSPCA too," Oliver said, as people began to move over to the stalls. "I don't think it's fair to keep the money after everything that's happened."

"That's a really nice idea, Oliver," Mandy agreed, as their first customers started crowding around.

"Those peanut-butter bones look tasty, Mandy," said Peter Foster, who was in her class at school. "Timmy will love those! I'll have two, please."

Mandy popped two bones in a paper bag, keeping her eye on the door. She wanted to be the first to catch a glimpse of the two special guests.

Just at that moment, she saw the door open, and in came Mandy's mum.

Mandy gasped. "James, look!"

By this time, everyone in the hall had turned to stare. Trotting quietly by her mum's side on a lead was an adorable baby goat, with a soft white coat. Mrs Hope was followed by Lydia Fawcett, leading another little kid just like the first one. Lydia owned a goat farm on the moor, just outside Welford.

"Aren't they lovely?" Mandy turned to her gran, her eyes shining. "This is brilliant!"

Her gran smiled. "Perhaps you and James would like to put this on the pen," she said, bringing out a sign she had kept hidden under the table.

Everyone was crowding round to pet the kids, who didn't seem at all nervous. Meanwhile, Mandy and James fixed the big sign to the front of the pen. Mandy took a step back to read it.

Our Two Kids Need a Name!
Can you think of names for Lydia's baby goats?
The best suggestion will win this wonderful
Christmas cake!
50p per suggestion

Mandy laughed. "So that's the competition!" she said, as Mrs Hope and Lydia Fawcett led the kids over to the pen. "What a good idea."

"Here we are, Mandy," beamed Lydia. "And I think we'd better get the kids into the pen before they attack all your goodies!"

Mandy laughed, reaching over briefly to feel the softness of their coats. The baby goats were already sniffing with interest at the huge Christmas cake. Lydia shooed them inside the pen, and a large crowd gathered round to read the sign.

"I've got a good idea," announced Peter Foster. "What about Holly and Ivy? That's really Christmassy."

"Well, I suppose the names don't *have* to be Christmassy," Mandy replied, glancing at her gran. "But it might be nice."

"What about Pudding and Pie?" suggested Reverend Hadcroft, who'd come over to see the kids. The two little goats were standing quietly in the pen, nibbling at some hay.

"Tinsel and Turkey," piped up little Libby Masters, blushing as everyone laughed.

"Here, write your suggestions down," Mandy said, handing round paper and pencils. "And put your name on the back."

"Lydia's going to choose the winner at the end of the fair," Gran explained. "Oliver, could you collect the 50ps, please?"

"Here's your Mum and Dad, Oliver," James said, spotting Mr and Mrs Morgan and Tammy walking across the hall.

"Oh, aren't the baby goats sweet?" exclaimed Mrs Morgan. "Shall we have a go at the competition, Tammy?"

Mandy handed her a piece of paper, and then began collecting all the suggestions in a large biscuit tin. It seemed as if everyone at the fair wanted to think of names for the kids. Mandy and Oliver were kept very busy, collecting suggestions and money. Meanwhile, James was doing a roaring trade in animal treats, and Gran and Grandad were rushed off their feet selling cakes at the other end of the table.

After two hours, almost everything on the stall had been sold. Gran and Grandad had just a few scones left, while all of the animal treats had vanished, except for a couple of bird cakes. James and Oliver started to collect up all the empty boxes.

"We've done really well!" Mandy said delightedly, looking at all the money they'd made. "Now we've just got to wait for Lydia to decide which names she likes." She reached into the pen and stroked the kids, who were curled up together with their legs tucked under them. "Well done, you two. You've helped to raise lots of money for the RSPCA."

"Hey, what's this?" James was burrowing under the table in one of the boxes. "Look, Mandy, I've found some more packets of hamster treats. We must have forgotten to put them out."

"Never mind." Mandy grinned at Oliver. "I know some hamsters who'll *love* them."

"When is Lydia going to announce the result of the competition?" Gran asked. "The fair's nearly over."

"Mum's given her the box with all the bits of paper in it," Mandy replied. "We're waiting for her to decide."

Just then Lydia came over to them. "I've chosen the winner," she said. "But I think *you* should be the one to announce it, Mandy."

"Me!" Mandy gasped.

"Well, your gran told me how patient you've been about her secret. You must have been dying to know who the surprise guests were! Lydia smiled and handed Mandy a piece of paper. "Go on, everyone's waiting."

Mandy hurried over to the platform. There were still lots of people left in the hall, and everyone clapped as she climbed the steps. Mandy cleared her throat. "The winning names for Lydia's kids are—' She looked down at the piece of paper. "Snap and Cracker." Everyone clapped again. "And the winner is . . ." Mandy turned the paper over, and smiled broadly. "Mrs Morgan!"

10

Hamster Christmas!

"Have you eaten all of Gran's Christmas cake yet, Oliver?" Mandy teased. It was later that evening, and she, Oliver and James were sitting in the living-room of the Hopes' cottage, waiting for the choir to arrive.

Oliver shook his head. "Not yet," he replied. "Mum says we can't have any till Christmas Day."

"I thought Snap and Cracker were brilliant names," James chimed in.

Just then, Mandy saw a group of people approaching the house carrying lanterns. "Look, here comes the choir." Mandy bounced excitedly out of her seat.

They all looked through the window, as the choir grouped round the door of the cottage and began to sing 'O Come All Ye Faithful'. It was a cold night, and there was a thick frost everywhere which sparkled and glittered in the light of the lanterns. Mandy thought the whole scene looked very Christmassy.

As the choir reached the last verse, Mandy's mum came into the living-room, carrying a large tray. "Mulled wine for the grown-ups, and hot chocolate with cream," she announced, putting the tray down on the coffee table. "I expect they're all frozen, poor things. Mandy, would you go and fetch the mince pies?"

Mandy nodded, and hurried off into the kitchen. When she came back with a large plate of mince pies, the members of the choir were

in the hall, taking off their coats and scarves.

"Mmm, they look good, Mandy." Mr Hope sneaked a mince pie off the plate and took a large bite. "Come in and get warm by the fire, everybody."

The choir crowded into the living-room. It was a bit of a squeeze, but nobody minded, not even Mrs Ponsonby. Mandy, James and Oliver handed round the hot drinks, and everyone took one gratefully.

"Where are the hamsters?" Amy Fenton asked, sipping her hot chocolate.

"They're in reception," Mandy replied. "That's the quietest place at the moment. Mum, shall we go and get them?"

Mrs Hope nodded, so Mandy, James and Oliver hurried through the door into the surgery. They came back, each carrying a cage.

"Here are the babies, Reverend Hadcroft," Mandy said, handing the cage over. "Charlie, Toffee, Biscuit, Peanut and Lulu."

"Goodness, I hope you don't expect me to tell them apart!" exclaimed the vicar. He peered into the cage. Everyone laughed when Charlie scampered right up to the bars, put his little nose between them and stared back at Reverend Hadcroft.

Then Oliver handed Frisky to Amy, who looked thrilled.

"It's almost as good as having my very own hamster," she said happily. "I shall put his cage next to Minnie's so he has someone to talk to."

James gave Milly to Mrs McFarlane, and then they went back for the others. Mr Raymond got Pinky and Billy, and Jean Knox and Kathy took Mungo and Barney.

They Mandy presented Herbert, in his plastic tank, to Mrs Ponsonby. "Herbert's a very special hamster," she explained. "He's a Roborovski, and he's too lively to live in an ordinary cage. But we thought you would like to have him."

Mrs Ponsonby looked pleased. "Well, thank you, Mandy," she said. "He's a cute little thing, I must say," she added, as Herbert popped his furry head out of his bedding and looked at her.

"I'll come and visit every day," Oliver told everyone. "Just to see how the hamsters are getting on."

Mandy smiled to herself. Everyone seemed very pleased with their new house guests. It looked like it was going to be a very merry Christmas for everyone, including the hamsters.

"Merry Christmas, Reverend Hadcroft!" Mandy announced with a smile. "We've got a special delivery for you."

It was Christmas morning. It had snowed the night before, but that hadn't stopped Mandy, James and Oliver from meeting up to visit the hamsters in their new homes. Mandy's dad had driven them out to Bleakfell Hall, where they'd found Herbert being pampered and petted with the tastiest vegetable treats by Mrs Ponsonby. Then they'd come back to Welford to see the others, and the vicarage was their last stop. All the hamsters seemed to have settled into their new homes perfectly.

"Merry Christmas to you all," Reverend Hadcroft beamed. Then he looked puzzled, as

Mandy handed him a neatly wrapped package. "What's this?"

"It's some of Mrs Hope's Christmas cake," Oliver explained. "Mum wanted to share it with all the people who are looking after hamsters for me."

"Well, that's very kind of her," Reverend Hadcroft replied. "I know how delicious Mrs Hope's cakes are. I hope you saved some for yourself?"

"Oh, we've got plenty left," Oliver assured him. "The cake was enormous!"

"And these are for the babies." Mandy handed over a packet of the hamster treats.

"How are they, Reverend Hadcroft?" James asked.

"They're fine." The vicar smiled and opened the door wider. "Would you like to come in and see them?"

They all went into the vicarage. The babies' cage was in Reverend Hadcroft's study, which was warm and cosy. Biscuit and Peanut were curled up together in their bed, and Charlie was running energetically round in the wheel.

Meanwhile, Toffee and Lulu were stuffing their cheeks with hamster mix.

"Here you are." Mandy opened a bag of hamster treats and took out a tiny piece of apple. She pushed it through the bars of the cage, and Toffee and Lulu both rushed over. Toffee got to it first, and began to crunch it happily.

"So have you been all over Welford this morning to visit the other hamsters?" asked Reverend Hadcroft.

Oliver nodded. "This really *has* been a

hamster holiday," he joked.

James grinned. "More like a hamster tour of Welford, you mean!"